MY COMMUNITY

A TRIP TO THE COMMUNITY GARDEN

Melissa Raé Shofner

PowerKiDS press.

New York

Published in 2017 by The Rosen Publishing Group, Inc.
29 East 21st Street, New York, NY 10010

First Edition

Editor: Melissa Raé Shofner
Book Design: Mickey Harmon

Photo Credits: Cover Jupiterimages/Getty Images; p. 5 Mark Bolton/Getty Images; p. 6 Steve Debenport/Getty Images; p. 9 Alistair Berg/Getty Images; p. 10 Viacheslav Nikolaenko/Shutterstock.com; p. 13 azure/Shutterstock.com; p. 14 Tobi Corney/Getty Images; p. 17 Blueguy/Shutterstock.com; p. 18 Ariel Skelley/Getty Images; p. 21 Nattapol Sritongcom/Shutterstock.com; p. 22 TunedIn by Westend61/Shutterstock.com.

Cataloging-in-Publication Data

Names: Shofner, Melissa Raé.
Title: A Trip to the community garden / Melissa Raé Shofner.
Description: New York : PowerKids Press, 2017. | Series: My community | Includes index.
Identifiers: ISBN 9781499427813 (pbk.) | ISBN 9781499430028 (library bound) | ISBN 9781508152927 (6 pack)
Subjects: LCSH: Community gardens–Juvenile literature. | Gardening–Juvenile literature.
Classification: LCC SB457.3 S56 2017 | DDC 635–d23

Manufactured in the United States of America

CPSIA Compliance Information: Batch #BW17PK: For Further Information contact Rosen Publishing, New York, New York at 1-800-237-9932

CONTENTS

Gardens grow food.

Everyone helps in the town garden.

We start planting in spring.

We plant peas.
We plant beans.

We even plant **corn**.

Gardens need water and sunlight.

Watch the garden grow!

We pick the food when it's ready.

There is so much to eat!

Everyone takes some home.

WORDS TO KNOW

corn

garden

INDEX

WEBSITES

Due to the changing nature of Internet links, PowerKids Press has developed an online list of websites related to the subject of this book. This site is updated regularly. Please use this link to access the list:
www.powerkidslinks.com/mycom/garden